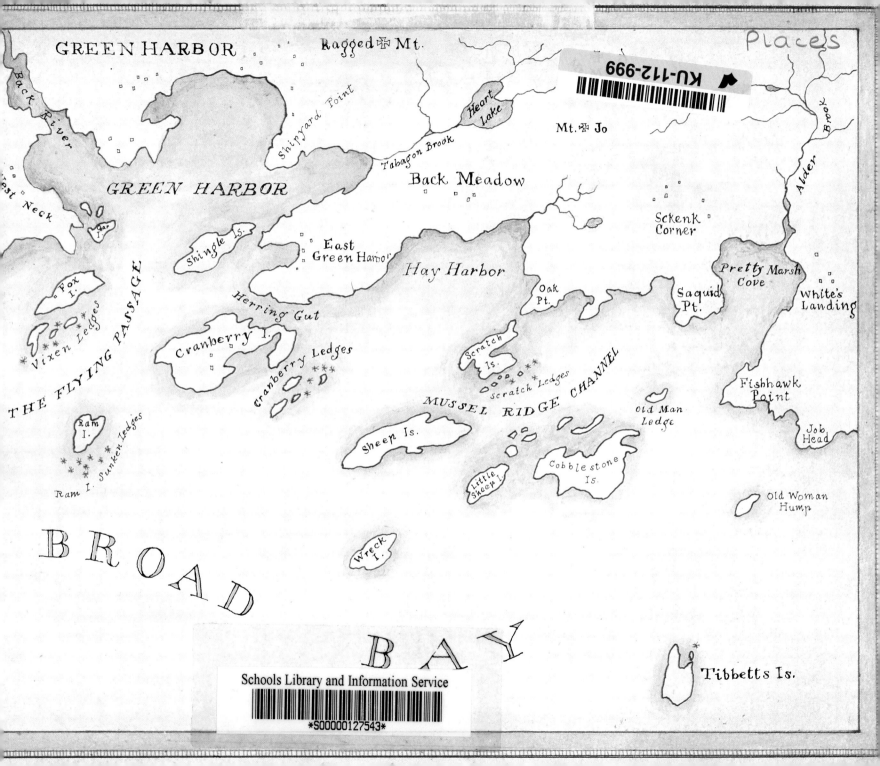

Places

GREEN HARBOR

Ragged ✠ Mt.

Back River

West Neck

GREEN HARBOR

Shipyard Point

Tabagon Brook

Heart Lake

Mt. ✠ Jo

Back Meadow

Alder Brook

Sckenk Corner

Shingle Is.

East Green Harbor

Hay Harbor

Pretty Marsh Cove

White's Landing

Fox I.

Vixen Ledges

THE FLYING PASSAGE

Herring Gut

Cranberry I.

Cranberry Ledges

Oak Pt.

Saquid Pt.

Scratch Is.

Scratch Ledges

MUSSEL RIDGE CHANNEL

Fishhawk Point

Ram I.

Ram I. Sunken Ledges

Sheep Is.

Old Man Ledge

Job Head

Little Sheep I.

Cobblestone Is.

Old Woman Hump

BROAD

Wreck I.

BAY

Tibbetts Is.

ISLAND BOY

Story and pictures by BARBARA COONEY

Julia MacRae Books   JM   A DIVISION OF WALKER BOOKS

Copyright © Barbara Cooney Porter, 1988
All rights reserved
First published in the U.S.A. 1988
by Viking Penguin Inc.
First published in Great Britain 1989
by Julia MacRae Books
A division of Walker Books Ltd
87 Vauxhall Walk, London SE11 5HJ

Printed in Italy by Lito di Roberto Terrazzi

British Library Cataloguing in Publication Data
Cooney, Barbara, *1917 –*
Island boy
1. Title
823′ . 914[J]
ISBN 0-86203-416-7

FOR TWO FRIENDS:

FOR RUTH & FOR EUGÉNIE.

At first there was just the island. It sat by itself, the outermost island, crowned with spiky spruce trees, facing the sea. Behind it, in the bay, lay the other islands, and behind them, the mainland and Green Harbour, where the family came from.

It was Pa who felled the trees and cleared the north end of the island. It was he who dug the well now full of sweet water. It was he who cut the stone and the wood to make the house. When all was ready, he brought his wife, the three children, and the family cow to live on the island. Henceforth it would be known as Tibbetts Island, for that was the family name.

Time passed. Now there were six boys and six girls, twelve children in all. From a beam in the loft hung an old sail, dividing the room in two. In the soft salt air wafting up from the cove, they slept, the girls on one side, the boys on the other. All, that is, except Matthais, the little clear-eyed quiet one, the baby. He slept in a trundle bed downstairs next to his mother and father.

Pa taught the boys to plough and to plant, to fell a tree and to build a stone wall. He taught them to cut ice and stone, to hunt and fish. And he taught them how to handle a boat.

Pa and the boys cleared more land, making room for potatoes and beans, for squash and corn and cabbages and onions. They built a shelter for their thirty sheep and a barn for the six cows and the two oxen, Star and Bright. They built a chicken house, a sty for the two pigs, and a fish house down in the cove. Matthais tagged along, always watching, always underfoot. "Go play somewhere," said his big noisy brothers. "You're too small to help."

"I'm not," said Matthais. So he went to help the girls collect eggs. Later, while they were milking, he sat under the red astrakhan apple tree Ma had planted above the house and thought about his smallness.

But he did not stay small forever.

Soon he was old enough to learn to read.

When the house had been banked with spruce boughs and the firewood cut for winter, the bitter cold came. Matthais would wake with the tip of his nose like ice. The window-panes frosted over, and the wind whistled in the chimney. Sea smoke hung over the open water. Then the children would crowd into the steamy kitchen, learning to read and write under Ma's fierce eye.

When they could bear the indoors no longer, they hung around the barn helping Pa with the animals. And when the snow crusted over they climbed the hill and slid down from the red astrakhan tree to the fish house.

"You *could* use a barrel stave," said Ma.

But the children preferred the seat of their pants.

As Matthais grew older, he worked side by side with his brothers, ploughing and planting and chopping wood. Soon he began to go out fishing with Pa. One sparkling morning the two set off. The Egg Rock, far to the west, was shining in the early light.

"What a handsome day it is!" said Pa. "Let's go get your ma some eggs. The hens ain't laying."

Despite a good breeze there was almost no swell, and Pa could pull in right alongside the Rock.

"I'll hold the boat here," he said, catching onto the rock with his gaff. "Get going, Matthais, and fill the basket with eggs."

Matthais scrambled up among the gulls and the terns, the cormorants and the eiders and the sea pigeons.

On the Rock were many eggs and broken shells. Among them lay a small ball of grey-brown fluff—a baby seagull.

"An orphan," said Matthais, tucking the little bird into the basket.

"You can't tame a wild bird," said Ma.

But Matthais did. He dug clams and gathered mussels for the little gull. The bird ate everything, even pie and doughnuts. His pin feathers sprouted; then real feathers came; soon he was full-grown.

Over and over again, Matthais threw the bird up into the air, teaching him how to fly. But the gull preferred to hop. So Matthais called him Toad.

Wherever Matthais went, Toad went. He watched Matthais split kindling. He squatted in the grass, his neck thrust out, following Matthais's every move as he hoed the potatoes. He hopped and flopped behind Matthais down to the little cobble beach where they picked up lobsters at low tide. When Matthais and Pa went out fishing, Toad crouched seasick in the bottom of the dory.

"He'd be happier flying," said Pa.

"Yes," said Matthais, dismally.

Then one foggy day, out near the Egg Rock, the gulls called to Toad, and Toad understood. He spread his wings, gave a hop or two and then, in a wavery way, he was aloft, going home.

One by one the Tibbetts children grew up and left the island—the girls to marry and the boys to work in the shipyard of Uncle Albion, Pa's brother in Green Harbour. Only Matthais was left with Ma and Pa on Tibbetts Island.

"You're too young to leave home," said the brothers. "You're still wet behind the ears."

But Matthais, who wondered what lay beyond Tibbetts Island, didn't listen. And indeed, his turn to leave came sooner than anyone expected.

In Green Harbour, Uncle Albion was building a handsome schooner. When it was finished, everyone from the islands and from the neighbouring villages came to the launching. The ship was named the *Six Brothers,* and when she sailed, Matthais went along as cabin boy.

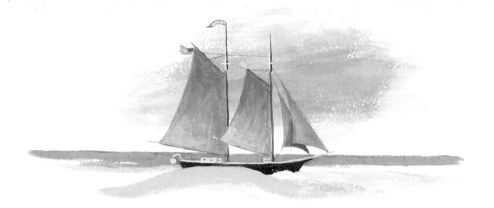

In every weather, Matthais sailed on the *Six Brothers* up and down the coast. From Green Harbour to Portland he sailed, to Boston, New York, and Philadelphia, even to the West Indies. The ship carried cobblestones gathered on the shores of the outermost islands—round ocean-smoothed stones to pave the city streets—and hay for the many horses that trotted about on those streets. The *Six Brothers* carried bricks from the brickyards along the tidal rivers for the elegant town-houses, and it carried heron and eider and gull feathers, to adorn the bonnets of the ladies who lived in those houses.

After fifteen years, Matthais, so steady, so clear-eyed, had become master of the *Six Brothers* and the pride of everyone in Green Harbour and around the bay.

But despite the bustle and wonders of the cities, Matthais could not forget the island. Whenever the *Six Brothers* entered the bay on a return voyage, when the Egg Rock came into view, and beyond it Tibbetts Island, Matthais's heart always skipped a beat. One day, Matthais told himself, I will return home.

And this he did.

On Matthais's last return voyage, the *Six Brothers* carried a young schoolmistress from Boston coming to teach in Graniteville. Her name was Hannah.

"No feathers on her bonnet," said Matthais approvingly.

Ma and Pa having moved to the mainland, the house on Tibbetts Island was empty. But the island was still home to Matthais. He used all the skills Pa had taught him: he repaired the roof of the house, jacked up the barn and the sheds, ploughed a patch for potatoes and corn. And in June he sailed up to Graniteville, where he married the schoolteacher Hannah and brought her home to the island.

Three little girls were born to Hannah and Matthais: Ellie and Nellie, the twins, and little Annie.

"A farmer needs sons for the heavy work," his brothers said. "You'd be better off on the mainland."

"No," said Matthais. "We belong here."

"And women and girls can work mighty hard too," said Hannah.

From June, when the scent of wild strawberries filled the air, until late summer, when the last of the raspberries, blackberries, and blueberries were gone, the girls went berrying. In the autumn, they gathered cranberries in the bog behind the sea beach. Then Hannah and the girls made jams and jellies, and pies as well from the apples of the red astrakhan tree.

Hannah taught the girls how to make butter and cheese, soap and candles, bread, Indian pudding, and a good chowder. They learned to spin and weave, to knit and sew—at least, Ellie and Nellie did.

But little Annie could not sit still indoors. She collected crabs and trotted behind Matthais when he wasn't off fishing. "My little wild bird," Matthais called her. She could whistle like one, too.

Time passed. The little girls grew up and went away. Even little Annie with the flyaway hair settled down and married a sail-maker. Matthais and Hannah remained on the island.

At about this time, people from away, from Boston and Philadelphia, discovered the beautiful bay. They bought up land near the water and built large houses that they called cottages. Along their docks they moored their pleasure boats. They called themselves rusticators.

"You could sell the island to the people from away," said Hannah.

"But our wants are so few now," said Matthais. "And this is home."

One winter, at the end of February, Hannah died, and Matthais was alone. He remembered her words about selling the island to the people from away. But no, he would not—need not—do that. Besides, now there was little Matthais to think of.

Every summer, Annie sent her son, little Matthais, out to the island. All day he followed his grandfather about. And at night he slept in the trundle bed, wrapped in the sweet air of the sea and the meadows. He wanted to stay on the island forever.

It was a cold hard winter, the year that little Matthais was five. The snow lay deep for months, and many people in Green Harbour died of the influenza. One was little Matthais's pa. That spring, Annie and little Matthais went out to live on the island for good.

In May, Matthais planted a much-too-big vegetable garden and had seven cows brought to the island.

"But we are just three people," said Annie.

"The people from away, the summer people, need vegetables," said Matthais. "And milk for their children, too."

Annie remembered all the things Hannah had tried to teach her. "Jellies and jams," she said. "And they will need their laundry washed and starched and ironed." For a while, anyhow, they were not going to sell Tibbetts Island.

Every day all summer Matthais and little Matthais loaded up the dory with cans of milk, with vegetables and eggs and butter, with jams and jellies, and hampers heaped with snowy linen, and set off across the bay towards the mainland.

In September, the people from away boarded up their houses and returned to the cities where the fathers worked and the children went to school. On the island, during the long winter evenings, Matthais and his grandson sat by the stove and played checkers and fox-and-geese. Sometimes Matthais told about life on Tibbetts Island when he was growing up. Sometimes he told wondrous tales about sailing on the *Six Brothers* and about life in the big cities.

"I too shall be a sea captain when I grow up," said little Matthais. "And then I will come back and live on Tibbetts Island."

"It is good to see the world beyond the bay," agreed old Matthais. "Then you will know where your heart lies."

"I already know," said little Matthais.

"Better to wait and see," said his grandfather.

For a long time, life continued in this peaceful way.

Then one morning late in August, old Matthais and young Matthais loaded the dory for a trip to the mainland. The weather was lowery and the wind in the southeast.

"It's going to blow. You keep to home today," said old Matthais to his grandson. Reluctantly young Matthais went back up the hill to the house.

Old Matthais did not come home that day. They never saw him alive again. Later they found the dory swamped—and Matthais nearby.

Boatloads of people in dark clothing came from all over to the funeral: sisters and brothers, nieces and nephews, boat-builders and storekeepers, men who had sailed and fished with old Matthais, saltwater farmers from the other islands and the mainland, even people from away. They came in boats of all sizes, hurrying before the northwest wind, to come to rest in the sheltered cove on Tibbetts Island.

The people climbed the hill and crowded into the little farmhouse to pay their respects to the steadfast old man of Tibbetts Island.

"A good man," young Matthais heard them say. "A good life."

And on that handsome day they buried old Matthais under the red astrakhan tree above the house.

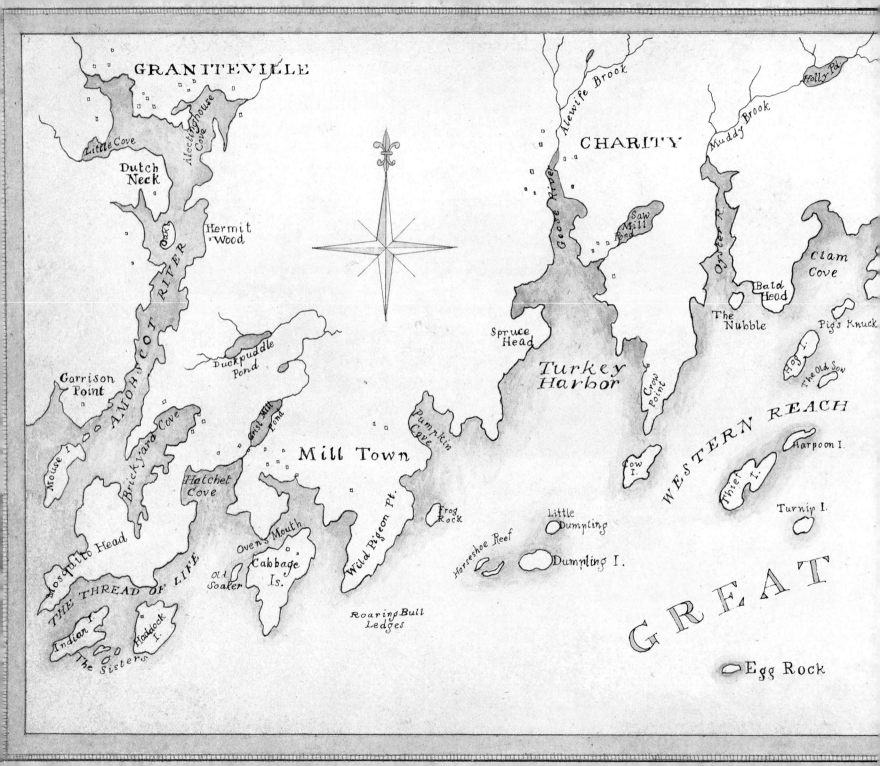